A Word of Warning

Burn for Jack is a dark monster romance novella containing graphic content not suitable for all audiences. Trigger warnings: graphic sex scenes, attempted sexual assault, bullying, gore/violence, breath play, blood play, bondage, and murder.

Also, note that this is a 21,000-word novella. If you're looking for something plot heavy, this may not be the book for you. If you're looking for a quick and spooky read about our heroine getting dicked down by a pumpkin-headed monster in a pumpkin patch, then read on...

AIDEN PIERCE

A HALLOWEEN MONSTER ROMANCE NOVELLA

Aiden Pierce

Burn For Jack

Copyright Aiden Pierce 2022
All Rights Reserved
First Published 2022

No part of this book may be reproduced, stores in a retrieval system or transmitted in any form by any means, without prior authorization in writing of the publisher, nor can it be otherwise circulated in any form of binding or cover other than that which it is published and without a similar condition, including this condition, being imposed on the subsequent purchaser. All characters and places in this publication other than those clearly in the public domain are fictitious, and any resemblance of actual persons, living or dead, is purely coincidental.

Cover Design: Opulent Swag and Designs
Editing: Killing it Write Editing Services
Formatting: Wicked Gypsy Designs

PLAYLIST

"Straight to Hell" – LVCRFT
"Season of the Witch" – Lana Del Rey
"Devil's Playground" – The Rigs
"When the Devil Calls My Name" – LVCRFT
"All the Good Girls Go to Hell" – Billie Eilish
"Whore" – In This Moment
"Devil Devil" – MILCK
"Death Couldn't Tear Us Apart" – LVCRFT

CHAPTER 1
ADA

A shrill scream pierced the autumn night.
Adrenaline pumped through me as I forced my feet forward, my ears ringing from the high-pitched scream.

"Derrick, knock it off, you prick!" Chelsea—one of my classmates—shrieked as she raced past us in her slutty little bunny outfit, drunkenly stumbling through the cornfield. One boy from our school ran after her, who was ironically dressed as a werewolf, pelting her with candy corn.

Just like the dozen other Hallow High students that had trekked to the town's pumpkin patch, they were drunk.

I was the only sober one. I was the only one who wasn't having any fun. But I was used to being the odd one out. You couldn't really avoid it when you came from a long line of witches so infamous we came with our own folktale. I mean, we weren't actual witches. Or if we ever were, it had been lost somewhere down the family line. The only thing my mother could brew was moonshine.

But since the New England witch craze, they've called the women in my family witches. With the most recent generations, they added a few more words. Outcast. Weirdo. Whore was the newest one, thanks to my drunk of a mother taking on a new occupation around town when my dad left. "Anything to pay the bills," she'd said the first time I'd found out from one of the cruel boys at school who'd seen her at his house, "entertaining" his father.

Someone nudged me in the ribs so hard I stumbled and had to catch myself. I glared up at the familiar face that leered at me, his dark eyes flashing malevolently from under the brim of his hat. "Fuck off, Lucas," I spat.

Lucas was the lead douche in what I'd coined "The Hallow Point Hicks," the ring of bullies who got off on making my life a living Hell. I was pretty sure most of them would leave me alone if it wasn't for this dick right here. He was still pissed about what happened on the first day of my freshman year. He'd cornered me behind the school, completely smashed and looking for something I wasn't selling.

He'd fucked with the wrong bitch on the wrong damn day and got his nose broken for the trouble. I was almost expelled, which was a total joke. I was the one who had to defend myself against a boy three years older and twice my body mass, all because he seemed to have an allergic reaction to the word no.

He had all the boys and some of the girls, too, calling me a whore the very next day. Oh, the fucking irony. I thought when he'd graduated two years ago, the torment would be over. But no. Lucas wasn't going to leave town for college. Instead, he stayed in Hallow Hill to work for his dad on his farm. All the senior boys still worshipped him. Being twenty-one, he could buy them all booze. To them, he might as well be God.

Lucas scoffed softly to himself, his vodka-rank breath making my stomach heave. I braced myself, ready to fight back if he decided to hit me. At least this time, there were witnesses. Most of them were assholes, but at least Chelsea would vouch for me if anything happened.

In my periphery, Derrick tackled a giggling Chelsea in the cornstalks. She playfully slapped him away and sat up, picking a piece of candy corn out of her hair. Her laughter died, and her eyes narrowed through her bunny mask when her attention landed on us. "Leave her alone, Luc."

"What? I'm not doing anything but offering her a drink." He shoved the bottle of vodka toward me, probably hoping I'd flinched when he moved just a little too aggressively. His lips flattened when I didn't so much as twitch. "Come on, Little Moore Whore. Don't you want to grow up to be just like mommy? Take a drink."

I bristled at the nickname. I wasn't going to be anything like my mother. I was going to do something no other Moore woman had done before me. Graduate and get the hell out of this town.

"I'm good, thanks," I said, brandishing a too-sweet smile. "I'm not here to get trashed. I'm here because I took your stupid bet. After tonight you're going to owe me two-hundred bucks. Hope daddy pays you enough for cleaning up pig shit to cough up."

The rest of my classmates gathered around us. Well, except for Chelsea and Derrick, who had laid back down, their tangled legs visible from behind a row of corn, where the sound of sloppy kissing was so loud it could be heard over the rustling stalks.

Everyone else had their attention on Luc, waiting to see what he'd do. His jaw flexed as his teeth ground audibly. Normally I wasn't the slightest bit afraid of the bully, but the fact that he was dressed up like Freddy Krueger had my heart racing. Not because his striped sweater or the half-assed makeup he'd applied was even sort of scary. It was because he'd made the leather glove out of real blades he'd found around his farm.

My mom had come home on a couple of occasions with a black eye and various other bruises. Luc's dad was one of her frequent customers, so I knew for a fact that he was a drunk who liked to beat up on women. The apple didn't fall far from the tree, so I wouldn't put it past Lucas to use his Krueger claw. One slash of that thing, and I'd be a goner.

"Look at Ada. She's scared shitless. She's white as a ghost," Derrick cackled, peering through the cornstalks. He omitted a loud "ouch," then dropped his voice. "Hey, what are you doing, babe?"

"Getting away from you. You're being a douche." A moment later, Chelsea emerged, her mask slightly askew with a few pieces of dried cornhusk sticking out from her mussed hair.

I turned my attention back to Lucas and dramatically rolled my eyes. "I look like a ghost because that's my costume, numb nuts," I snarled at him.

Chelsea walked back over to us, straightening her mask. "You guys are all assholes. She already took the bet to go to the patch on Halloween. Did you really have to make her dress up as her ancestor? Kind of disrespectful, if you ask me."

"How's it disrespectful?" someone challenged. I didn't look to see who said it. I was too busy holding Luc's lethal glare with one of my own.

Lucas stared at me with unflinching hatred. "Because the very first witch in the Moore family died on this night hundreds of years ago. After that, no Moore woman dared go to the pumpkin patch until Ada's great-great-grandmother over a hundred years ago. She came back down, totally naked and completely insane, babbling about a pumpkin-headed devil. She got shipped off to the loony bin, and no one ever saw her again. So it seems Halloween isn't a good night for the Moores."

Luc's gloved fingers curled around the neck of the vodka bottle, his metal claws clinking against the glass as he put it to his lips and took a big swig. He hissed through clenched teeth, vodka dribbling down his chin. "Thing is. I don't give a shit. No one made Ada take the bet. No one made her come. It's not like anyone would blame her for not coming. Especially since Pumpkin Head has a thing for the Moore Whores."

I cringed, but not at the cruel name he used for me. For some reason, it didn't sit right with me whenever anyone referred to Jack Calloway as Pumpkin Head. Maybe it was because I felt sorry for him on some level, even if he died hundreds of years ago. Sure, the town called him a monster. Not because he was literally a monster. He was a male witch, but from the story, his only crime was his wild sex life with my ancestor, Adaline Moore—the woman I was named after.

Neither of them deserved what had happened.

I shivered as a chill that had nothing to do with the crisp fall night crawled into my bones. I couldn't shake the feeling that I had no business being here on this night, of all nights. That maybe I should have listened to them when they said to stay away from the pumpkin patch on Halloween night.

Derrick was right. No one made me come. I'd taken the stupid dare to dress up like my ancestor, wearing a period dress of the time, and make this trek to the pumpkin patch on All Hallows' Eve. The challenge was that when Jack didn't show, that would prove there was no such thing as ghosts, as I repeatedly claimed.

I had to ignore the little alarm bells going off in my mind, so I could shut everyone else up and prove to them once and for all there was no pumpkin-headed specter haunting the town's pumpkin patch, waiting for the return of Adaline Moore.

It was almost too bad I didn't believe in ghosts.

There was nothing for me here in this shit town with these shit people.

I almost wished Jack Calloway was real, so he could take me far away from this shit hole.

Wherever he'd take me, even if it was Hell itself, it had to be better than here.

Chapter 2
Ada

Hallow Hill got its name because of the large hill that rose over everything, with the town sitting at the bottom of one end and a densely wooded area flanking the other side. At the very top was the pumpkin patch, along with a narrow cornfield that ran along the side of the hill and stretched all the way to town, acting as a sort of privacy screen.

Derrick grabbed a husk of corn, twisted it from its stalk and hurled it at another guy. He was as sloshed as the rest of them and too slow to dodge it even though he was the school's star quarterback for the football team. It bounced off his shoulder and smacked Lucas in the head.

Luc whirled around and stomped toward Derrick with his eyes practically aglow with fury. "Don't make me regret leaving you back in town to trick or treat with the rest of the kiddies."

Ignoring his friend's frantic apology, Lucas seized a fistful of Derrick's flannel werewolf get-up and hauled him so close their noses practically touched.

"I'm sorry, Luc! It was an accident!" he babbled.

"Kiss," I jeered. As much as he got under my skin, I did my best not to provoke Lucas. It just made life easier when I flew under his radar ninety percent of the time. But there were times, mostly when he turned his anger on other people, that I couldn't keep my mouth shut. Especially when Derrick managed to stir up a shred of pity for himself, cowering the way he was.

Just as I hoped, the alpha bully swerved his attention back to me as he appeared to be deliberating who'd take his ire this time. He backed off entirely—probably because people were watching—and laughed it off like his drunken abuse was some joke. "Better watch out, Chels. Looks like our little Moore Whore has a thing for your man."

Derrick pulled his shirt from Luc's slackened grip and tugged his girlfriend into his arms, chuckling nervously. "Y-yeah, right. I wouldn't touch that pussy with a ten-foot pole. Who knows where it's been."

Funny since I was a virgin. Not that any of this trash needed to know that.

Chelsea was the only one not laughing. Her attention was still on me, sending me an apologetic look as she mouthed "thank you" under the rim of her half-bunny mask. She knew I'd just saved her boyfriend a bruise or two. She also wasn't blind and knew I was the one who wouldn't touch Derrick Randle with a ten-foot pole, even if he was the last guy on earth. That went for all the Hallow High Hicks.

In elementary school, Chelsea and I had been friends. Then she got with Derrick in middle school, and he was a package deal. She had to pick sides. Me or her boy toy and the rest of the Hallow hillbillies.

She didn't pick my side. No one ever did. Which was fine. It would only make leaving this place easier the moment I had that diploma in my hand. And that two hundred bucks Lucas would owe me after I debunked this ghost story. It would be enough for a bus ticket out of the state.

When we arrived at the top of the hill, everyone took a collective breath. It was so...beautifully eerie. The moon peeked out from the cloud cover, making the thin blanket of fog over the pumpkin patch glow.

After weeks of the patch being open to the town, this year's harvest was still mostly untouched. People would visit the patch, especially outsiders. With the folktale attached to it, the pumpkin patch was Hallow Hill's only attraction that pulled in outsiders. But few people ever bought the pumpkins. Some people believed Jack Calloway's curse poisoned everything that grew from the grounds where he died and that his pumpkins carried a piece of him. So taking his property was asking for bad juju, let alone carrying it into your home and defiling it with one of those cheesy pumpkin decorating kits.

Chelsea was one of the few people in town who wasn't put off by it. "Oh my God!" she squealed and scurried over to one of the larger pumpkins in the field. "This is the biggest squash I've ever seen!"

Derrick snickered. "Where have I heard that before?"

Ignoring the dick joke, Chelsea pulled out her phone and pranced to the middle of the patch, where a stack of haybales sat. Next to the bales was the pumpkin patch's scarecrow.

Hallow Hill's scarecrow was different than what you'd find in other crops. It wasn't there to scare crows but to appeal to the tourists who would come here. The scarecrow had a jack-o'-lantern for a head, with a sinister grin and mean eyebrows. Instead of being propped on a stake, it was locked inside some worn stockades that had belonged to the town since back when they were still using these things.

Chelsea posed next to the scarecrow and snapped a selfie. She glanced at the screen, approving the picture with a satisfied hum and shoved her phone back into her pocket. "Cool. So we're here. What now? Isn't pumpkin head supposed to be here or something?"

I turned to Lucas and stuck out my hand, curling my fingers to signal, "gimme," and added a smirk. "Yeah, cough up, asshole."

"We just got here," Lucas growled.

"I'm not going to wait all night."

"If you want your money, you're gonna wait as long as I fucking say."

I folded my arms over my chest, shooting him a withering glare. "Then what are we supposed to do exactly?"

Lucas turned to one of his friends, who had a half-eaten candy bar in his hand. "You bring it?"

Candy Bar gave a jerk of a nod as he shrugged his backpack from his shoulder, probing inside it with one hand while taking a bite of his candy with the other. I expected him to pull out another bottle of booze or something. Maybe weed or cigarettes.

When he extracted a Ouija board instead, I groaned. "Oh, you gotta be kidding me."

"Sit the fuck down," Lucas instructed. Everyone did as they were ordered, sitting in a circle with the board placed in the center.

When I remained standing, Lucas jabbed a bladed finger at me. "You too."

"Yeah, right. I wore the stupid costume. I showed up. That was the deal. You said nothing about a fake ass little séance."

Lucas was so angry he looked like he was ready to spew lava. I held my ground, folding my arms over my chest to show him I wasn't backing down. I never did, and I never would. Maybe one day, he'd get that through his stupidly thick skull.

After a few awkward beats, he growled a "Fine. Watch then," and sat down in the circle.

Everyone had to squeeze in tight to place their fingers on the heart-shaped wooden piece.

"Shut the fuck up, assholes," Lucas snarled. Everyone immediately quieted. Even Candy Bar—Kyle was his name—stopped his chewing. "I saw a tutorial on YouTube. I think we need to move the planchette to warm it up..." Their arms all moved, and the wooden piece slid around in small circular motions.

"Wow. Luc's done some homework. Funny how that seemed to be beyond you in school, where it actually mattered."

Ignoring me, Lucas asked his first question. "How many spirits are present?"

"This is stupid," I muttered to myself, plopping down on one of the hay bales beside the scarecrow.

Since there were too many cooks in the kitchen as far as the Ouija board went, there was some awkward shuffling of the planchette before it was guided to the row of numbers.

"One," Chelsea gasped.

"Oh, for the love of God, this is—" I didn't finish my grousing. Lucas hurled his bottle of vodka at me. I flinched away just in time as it slammed against the hay bale with enough force to shatter it. I blinked at the broken glass at my feet in complete disbelief. "What the actual fuck? You could have seriously hurt me, you psychopath!"

Everyone gaped at Lucas, totally stunned by his outburst. No one spoke up. No one said *shit*. They were all anxiously eyeing the cruel weapon strapped to his hand.

Lucas went on to ask the board another question as if nothing had happened. "Are you a good spirit?"

There was more shuffling. "N," someone said.

"O," another breathed a second later.

No.

I suppressed the urge to shiver. This wasn't real, so of course, the answer was the one Luc wanted to hear. He was guiding the planchette.

"What's your name?"

"J."

"A."

"C."

"K."

I shot to my feet, glass crunching beneath my sneakers. "Okay. I'm over this. This doesn't count as him showing up, Lucas. He needed to actually *show up*. Give me the fucking money you owe me."

Luc met my gaze and opened his mouth, but instead of any response to me, what came out instead was another damn question. "And what do you want?"

This time, there was a longer pause before everyone moved the planchette across the board.

"A.

"D.

"A."

"You know what. Forget it." I flipped Lucas off before storming away, angrily kicking at the hem of my dress as I stomped through the pumpkin patch. "Should have known you weren't gonna stick to the deal."

"Grab her!"

"Wait, wha—"

The next thing I knew, several sets of hands grabbed me and dragged me back toward where Lucas sat. I fought against them, biting and scratching, but the boys were stronger than me. They threw me at Luc's feet, who regarded me with an expression on his face that made my blood freeze in my veins. "You know why I wanted you to come here tonight, Ada?"

Every muscle in my body tightened because I pretty much knew the answer.

"I want to watch you get taken by Pumpkin Head. Then there will be one less whore in town, running her mouth."

CHAPTER 3
ADA

Okay. So as thick-skinned as I was, that last line hurt. I mean, I already knew that he believed in the story. He really thought a pumpkin-headed spirit haunted the hill and that it was after the Moore women.

Almost everyone in town believed it. The fact that my great-great-grandmother had gone up the hill and gone back down with her marbles missing, rambling on about how some pumpkin monster had touched her, was proof enough for them. The only authentic part of that story was that my grandma had gone insane that night, which explained where the rest of her story came from.

I'd have to see the spirit of Jack Calloway myself before I bought into the story. But I had to admit to myself that it was stupid to come. Not because there was any real chance of getting kidnapped by supernatural forces, but because I knew Lucas was out for blood. And I had taken his bet anyway.

I'd been so desperate to prove to him that ghost stories, especially this one, were only that. Stories. The guy needed a serious reality check. I thought winning that money from him would be a great start. Then, maybe I'd break his nose. Just to remind him of the good old days and how I'd never be his to fuck with. But as per usual, things didn't go my way.

I spat on his feet, then lifted my gaze to his, forcing my signature "eat-shit-and-die" smile.

"I hope your tiny dick gets caught in your overall zipper, you back hills hick."

With my heart in my throat, I kicked my leg out and brought the heel of my foot down on his kneecap. He crumpled with a cry. Not wasting a second, I bolted to my feet and took off running.

"Don't let her get away!" Luc's voice came out pained and angrier than I'd ever heard it before.

Several footsteps thundered after me. I didn't dare look behind me, in case it slowed me down, but by the barrage of footsteps, at least three boys were on my tail.

Fuck. Fuck. *Fuck.*

I'd been the center of the Hallow Hill Hick's cruelty before but never like this. This was different. Before, it was all verbal. Name-calling, maybe the occasional lewd crayon hand-drawing one of them did depicting me fucking all of them, taped to the classroom whiteboard before the teacher could tear it down. They'd never put their hands on me before. Something told me tonight was the night they'd cross that line.

So I ran harder than I ever had before.

My heart thrashed in my chest, its beat roaring in my ear.

Maybe I could lose them in the cornfield. If I could make it that far. Just a few more feet— Yes!

I flung myself into the cornfield and sprinted between the row of stalks, careful not to touch them so they wouldn't give away my location. But my careful effort not to touch the stalks was all for freaking nothing when the tip of my shoe caught on the hem of my dress. I never *ever* wore dresses, and if it hadn't been for Lucas making it a part of the bet, I would never have worn this one. Yet another mistake.

I went hurtling to the ground, the cornstalks softening my

blow somewhat. Before I had enough time to pick myself up, they were on me.

One grabbed my flailing arms and pinned them over my head. Another sat on my legs, and a third straddled my hips.

"G–get off me!" I half shrieked, half growled, my voice coming out like something demonic. I bucked savagely, trying to free myself, but the boy on top of me clamped his knees tighter around my hips.

"Come on, Little Moore Whore. We're just helping you ease into the family business," he cackled, his breath reeking of liquor. He fumbled with the hem of my dress, trying to wrench it up, awkwardly distributing his weight so he could work it over my hips while he tried to remain on top of me.

My mind fractured. This wasn't happening. "St–stop! No!"

A fourth Hick broke through the cornstalks, and it took a moment for me to register the face. Derrick.

His face twisted in disgust. "Guys. What the hell? Get off her! This isn't what we're here to do."

An overwhelming wave of relief washed over me. So Derrick wasn't totally fucked up like the rest of Luc's demented crew. A barbed silence settled in, my three captors freezing. They looked between them, wordlessly asking, "Do we listen to this guy?"

My gut churned violently.

Derrick stomped forward and kicked the boy on top of me so hard he went sailing off me and skidding an entire row down in a spray of dirt. My savior shot a warning look at the other two, and they released me.

"Take her back to Luc."

"J–Just let me go!"

Derrick crouched, grabbed my arm and hauled me up with an apologetic look pinching his features. "Sorry."

An icy, hollow filling settled in my chest. *Sorry.*

I was sorry too. Sorry that I had been born into this town that was more like a disease than an actual home. A place where the people treated me like I was nothing but a cheap toy to toss around until I broke.

Wrangling me back to the pumpkin patch took longer than it should have, with me fighting every step of the way.

When Lucas and the rest of the group came into view, a chill swept down my back. A raven cawed somewhere in the distance. Dead leaves from the nearby wood crunched underfoot as I was marched to what felt like a trial.

Or an execution.

Lucas regarded me like I was trash. Worse than trash. "Put her in the stocks."

"What? No!" I screamed so loud a few nearby birds took flight. But it was useless. We were too far away from town for anyone to hear me.

"Guys, stop," Chelsea said, tugging at Derrick's sleeve in hopes he'd listen.

He didn't. Shocker.

This had been the plan all along.

They had to be planning on putting me in the stockade the whole time—they were too coordinated for this to be spur-of-the-moment.

One of them already had the stocks open, with the scarecrow dumped on the ground. Kyle was rummaging in his backpack again, shoving the Ouija board in and pulling a padlock out in its place.

They wrestled me into the stocks, forcing my neck into the biggest of the three holes, followed by my wrists into the smaller ones on either side of my head while Lucas stood in front of me, watching through a smile.

"You look so at home in that position. Bent over. Looking so scared and helpless."

I cringed. "Go to Hell!"

My heart dropped to my stomach when the top piece of wood locked into place and the padlock latched. I was trapped, at their complete mercy.

The boy who'd held my arms down in the cornfield came up behind me to grope my ass. Lucas screamed at him to back away, his bloodshot eyes flashing dangerously. "Keep your hands off of her. We're leaving her for Pumpkin Head."

Shit. He really was insane. But it's not like I was complaining. His steadfast belief in the pumpkin-headed spirit was literally keeping me from getting molested.

The bully stepped toward me and crouched so we were at eye level. "He's going to come for you, Ada. Have you imagined what he's going to do to you? I sure have. I think he's going to tear your pussy apart."

Chelsea came to my rescue then, or at least tried to. "Luc. Stop. You're scaring her."

She was the one he was scaring going by her sheepish whisper that wouldn't have made an obedient dog obey, let alone a feral mongrel like Lucas.

Pushing away the intense sensation winding through me, I gathered my nerves the best way I knew how. Mouthing off. "Yeah, yeah. It's no secret you like imagining me being fucked, Luca Lou," I taunted, knowing his mom's pet name for him would rile him. Especially since his mom pulled the same card as my dad and ran out on her family when Luc was barely out of elementary school.

"But I am surprised that you just admitted you imagine me getting railed by Pumpkin Head and not you. If you're into freaky stuff like that, who knows what kind of weird shit you get up to on that farm of yours? You know, with all those pigs and sheep..."

You could cut the tension with a pitchfork.

Lucas was so pissed his non-gloved hand shook as he shoved it into his pocket and fumbled for a lighter. It took several swipes of his thumb on the striker before the flame sprung to life and illuminated his Freddy Krueger makeup in an amber glow. "You better pray Pumpkin Head leaves nothing left of you, Adaline Moore. You better *pray*."

CHAPTER 4
ADA

"Uh...so what now?" Chelsea whined, rubbing her arms to stir some warmth into her scantily bunny-clad form. "I'm freezing my ass off."

"We wait," Luc gritted.

"For how long?"

"For as long as it takes for Pumpkin Head to show up." Luc waved his lighter around so the glow bathed the underside of his face. "Tell us a story, Adaline. Tell us the tale of Jack Calloway."

I gave a pained groan. Not because the stocks hurt. But because we'd all heard the legend of Jack Calloway three hundred million times. When every other kid in Connecticut grew up on Mother Goose and Grimm fairytales, we grew up listening to the same damn folk legend. We all knew it forward and back.

"Yeah, I'm gonna pass. Not really in the mood to swap ghost stories, you psycho."

Everyone shifted uncomfortably when Luc lifted his hand, the moonlight bouncing off the bladed claws of his Freddy Krueger glove.

Chelsea stepped forward. "I'll tell the story."

"I want Ada to do it," Luc drunkenly slurred. He shoved the lighter toward me, and his lips quirked when I flinched away from the flame. "I want to hear her tell the story of her whore ancestor."

"J–Jack Calloway was a witch. So was my ancestor, the first Adaline Moore. They had freaky sex and got discovered. Burned for witchcraft. Then the fire destroyed everything, and it's said that he still haunts the pumpkin patch to this day, waiting for the soul of his lover to return to him. The end. Now let me go."

"No," Luc snarled low in his throat. "Tell the whole story. The way your family tells it."

A cold sweat beaded my brow. He was doing his best to embarrass me, to strip me of all my dignity. But I came from witches. We were used to this shit. All he was doing was pissing me off.

He wanted a story? Fine. I'd give them the story as I knew it because, in the Moore household, the story was told differently. It was a tale of romance, loss and heartbreak. Of hope.

To everyone else, it was just a stupid ghost story.

"Once upon a time, long ago, there was a woman with hair the color of flames, skin as pale as the moon, and a soul that shone brighter than both. Adaline Moore was the village's greatest beauty, and they feared her. They feared her outspoken nature, her untamed heart, and her inability to be controlled. They said she'd never find a man who could hold her heart and keep its beat to himself. Until she met Jack Calloway, a sinfully handsome man who could charm the pants off a catholic priest if he had half a mind to."

I took a pause for dramatic effect. All eyes were on me, riveted. Just as I'd thought, no one had heard the story quite like this before. The version where Jack and Ada weren't the villains.

"Jack saw the wild woman for what she was. Fierce, radiant

freedom. In her arms, he found escape from the cruel world of those days. He nurtured her flame, encouraged her wicked words and worshiped her serpentine curves. When others told her to cover up, he told her to show more of her beauty. When they told her to keep her mouth shut, he urged her to speak louder. That didn't sit right with the townspeople in the age of the witch craze, where people burned strong women out of fear."

"That's not how—"

"Who's telling the story here, Luca Lou?" I smiled sweetly, brushing off the fire in his glare. "Anyway, the two were magic together. Living in their own perfect world, perfectly in love. Perfect bliss. They met every night under the full moon in the woods behind the hill, and one night, they were followed. The witness saw them making love—" My words shriveled in my throat with the breathy gasp that took their place when Luc surged forward, gripping my hair. He wrenched my head back, making the wood of the stockade dig painfully into my nape.

"Make love?" he seethed in a vodka-laced rasp. "Is that what you call what they did that night? Jack Calloway gutted a goat, smeared its blood over his naked whore, and swore her to the devil by writing the contract in runes on her bare tits and thighs. Is that your idea of a romantic time, Ada?"

I narrowed my eyes. "You're wrong. It was no contract to the devil. It was a vow to her. A poem."

My eyes fanned shut, and I breathed slowly to steady my rioting heart. In all honesty, I used to love Ada and Jack's grim love story. It was passed down through the women in my family, and the memories of being tucked in my bed with my mom reciting the poem were some of the only happy memories I had of her.

"Forever mine, wild vixen, her hair as bright as fire.
Forever mine, her sinful figure, forever my desire.

Forever mine, her wicked mouth, bold and bravely brash.
Forever mine, forevermore, through dust and darkest ash."

I opened my eyes, brandishing a smirk that I sent straight through Lucas. "Then it's said that Jack summoned spirits of the forest forward to witness his treasure and watch as he worshipped her body with his. So yeah. I think that's pretty romantic. Maybe you would too if you back hills hicks weren't so disgustingly vanilla."

"Spoken like a true whore," Luc mumbled, releasing his hold on my hair.

Now that I was invested in telling my version of the story, especially knowing it was pissing off Luc, I continued. "The next day, they were burned as witches on the edge of the pumpkin patch. With his last screaming breaths, Jack Calloway pledged himself to Satan so long as he saved his beloved's soul. Some say the devil answered because the fire broke out, consuming everything. When the flames cleared, his body was burned to a crisp, but Adaline Moore's body was nowhere to be found. Now, on the night the veil between our realms is the thinnest, Jack waits in the pumpkin patch where he saw her last, awaiting her return."

"You forgot the last part," Luc scoffed. "Your great-great-grandmother was the first Moore to come to the hill on Halloween night after that day. When she came back down, she was naked and insane, bawling about a pumpkin-headed spirit who thought she was his lost Little Moore Whore and tried to take her out for a spin. That or he knew it wasn't her and just decided that any Moore with red hair and a smart mouth would do. A ginger cunt is a ginger cunt."

I balled my hands into fists. They were so close to my ears I could hear my knuckles crack.

Maybe I wasn't as thick-skinned as I thought. Before, I would have been satisfied in taking Luc's money and rubbing it in his face by winning the bet. Maybe I'd call him stupid for believing in ghost stories. He'd say something out of line, and I'd throw a punch. I'd never forget the crunch of cartilage and the spurt of crimson when I'd broken his nose freshman year. I would have been happy with revenge like that.

But now? Now I'd be quite happy if the dumb fuck set himself on fire.

Watch anyone so much as breathe the words fire, witch, or whore, around me ever again.

"What did I ever do to you, Lucas? That day in freshman year—when I was *fifteen,* by the way, and you were eighteen—and you told me I had to fuck you or you'd make me, and I broke your nose for it, was your pride really so hurt? I was fifteen, you piece of shit. *Fifteen.* Three and a half years later, I'm still paying for standing up for myself. I've asked myself why. What could I have done differently? But you know what the answer is? Nothing. I wasn't in the wrong. You're trash, Lucas. You're nothing but trash. And I'm not. You see that, and you want me. But you can't have me because you're not good enough for me. And you and your tiny dick and your fragile as fuck ego can't handle that."

The sound of flesh striking flesh rang in my ears before the sting set in. He's slapped me across my face. He'd done it with his gloveless hand, which would have been preferable if it wasn't for the lighter he held. It wasn't one of those cheap disposable ones that would turn off when your thumb left the lever, either. It was the kind where the wick would stay ignited until the cap was closed.

So when the flame passed under my chin, I prepared for the pain. If anything, the only sensation was a faint brush of the flame tips as it tickled my face.

What the...Why didn't it hurt?

The flame had touched me. I know it did. So why hadn't I felt it?

Confusion transformed into unholy terror when the top of the lighter knocked against my chin and went tumbling from Luc's hand.

It was like one of those slow-motion moments in movies where shit was about to go up in flames.

In this case, shit really was about to go up in flames. Literally.

He'd thrown the vodka bottle at the hay bales earlier, which were just a few feet away. Enough for the alcohol to seep into the hay in a few-foot radius. So the moment the lighter smacked the ground at my feet, everything exploded in a flash of malevolent yellow and white fire.

It licked up the stockades, spreading over my clothes.

This was it.

This was how I'd die.

At almost the same spot where the first Adaline Moore was burned at the stake. It was almost poetic in a twisted way.

I screamed. On instinct. Not because it hurt.

It didn't hurt.

Wait...How was that possible? I was on freaking fire! How could it not hurt?

I couldn't make out anyone else through the wall of fire and the screen of smoke that separated me from the group.

Only one face was discernable through the flames. Luc's. He stood unmoving. Thunderstruck.

All color drained from his face as he watched the fire eat at the fabric of my dress while leaving my skin beneath unscathed.

I'd be naked in seconds. I was too stunned to care. I wasn't burning. I was literally on fire, and I was totally fine. Physically, anyway. My mental state was another story.

Chelsea's screams reached me through the fire. "Get her out, Lucas! Derrick! Anyone, before she burns!"

Then her scream took on a different pitch when she realized I was already on fire, totally fine in the wake of its infernal kiss.

What. The. Actual. Fuck.

My mind was racing to come up with some logical explanation for this. I drew a blank.

It was true.

Nope. That was impossible. Just because I seemed to be just a tad fire-resistant didn't mean magic was real. It didn't mean that... My train of thought disintegrated into ash when I realized the fire from the stockades had spread.

Everyone else had run for safety, leaving Lucas and me alone in the flames.

The fire shot across the dense tangle of pumpkin vines, creating a twisting maze fitting Hell itself.

I was immune to the flames for some freakish reason, but something told me Lucas wouldn't be. "Get out of here, now!"

Shock seemed to have a hold over his limbs because, for a moment, he didn't move. "You are a fucking witch. One that can't burn...You know what that means? It's all real. *He's* real." His voice changed, morphing into something intensely dark. "I'd give anything to watch him tear you apart."

"Would you give your life, you fucking idiot?" I screeched at him, rattling the stockades in the hope they'd crumble under the heat of the flames. Just like me, they remained untouched. "Because that's what's going to happen if you stay here a second longer."

It's not like I cared if the leader of the Hallow Hill Hicks died. I meant what I said. He was trash, and the time I had remaining in this miserable town would be so much more bearable with him gone.

I wanted him to get the hell out of here because, for the first time, I was questioning everything I knew about the story of Jack Calloway. If a ghost really was coming for me, who knew what he was going to do with me. Whatever it was, I didn't want Lucas to watch. So I sighed with relief when he finally turned and disappeared through the flames.

Leaving me for dead. Or worse.

CHAPTER 5
ADA

I was supposed to be dead.

But I was still breathing. I wasn't even burned.

The fire had crept away from me to the rest of the pumpkin patch, leaving me cold and shivering. It was almost funny how I missed being on fire. Then again, it hadn't felt like fire at all. The sensation was almost familiar, like slipping into a hot bath.

Even though there was no pain, a part of my animal brain screamed for me to run. Because I was still in danger.

I struggled against the stockade, the frame rattling dangerously but remaining sturdy. Weird. It should have been nothing but dust by now.

Then again, I should be nothing but dust, I reminded myself.

While the wooden stockade and my body locked inside it had remained untouched by the fire, my clothes were nothing but cinder and smoky pieces of fabric barely clinging to my curves.

A sweltering sensation washed over me, and again, it had nothing to do with all the fire. This had to be a nightmare. That explained it. A freakishly realistic nightmare.

Any moment I'd wake up. Just any moment now...

I flexed my eyes shut and recited Jack Calloway's poem out loud, only as the Moore women knew it.

I never cared about the portion of the legend where he made a deal with the devil and became a pumpkin-headed monster. I mean, the story *did* appeal to me. Just not in the way it did for other people. To me, it wasn't a scary bedtime story that haunted my nightmares.

Everyone else thought what Jack had done to Ada in the forest was depraved and sinister. Well, okay, so did I. But how was that a bad thing? He'd loved her. He really loved her by letting her be her wild, witchy self. And then he'd fucked her like an untamable Moore woman ought to be fucked.

There was a reason Jack Calloway and Adaline Moore had gone down in history. In Hallow Hill, being boring was pretty much a way of life. That went for vanilla sex, too. Which was why I was still a virgin—despite Luc's efforts.

The guys I was interested in didn't exist outside the world of make-believe. So Jack's poem had become something of an escape for me, and I held it close to my heart even though sometimes I wasn't sure why.

"Forever his, wild vixen, my hair as bright as fire." A gust of warm breeze fanned over me, making my red hair sway around my bare shoulders.

"Forever his, my sinful figure, forever his desire." The heat swelled between my legs, this time like a lover's caress. My heart hammered in the back of my throat, and I kept going, feeling something new compel me to finish the poem. Something that made the tiny hairs on the back of my neck stand.

"Forever his, my wicked mouth, bold and bravely brash."

A twig snapped, so close I could hear it over the crackling fire that raged through the pumpkin patch. I scanned the area as best I could, which was barely at all since the stockade around my neck restricted most of my movement.

My breath froze in my lungs when my attention landed on something else.

The scarecrow that had been dumped on the ground was now headless. The jack-o'-lantern was gone. My heart rate launched into light speed. Where did it go? It's not like it had burned up, not when the rest of its body was still lying there. And it's not like it just rolled away.

My entire body locked with fear, paralyzed as a wave of warmth rolled down my slightly curved spine, feathering over my flesh. It wasn't the gust of fire warmth. By the pummeling rush, wave after wave of hot air, I knew it was the prickly heat of hot breath.

Someone or something was behind me.

"Who—who's there? Luc, if that's you..." My voice broke. I already knew that it wasn't Lucas. It wasn't anyone I knew. No one breathed like that. Huge, cavernous, sweltering. As if they had two furnaces strapped together and mounted inside them in place of lungs.

"Forever mine, forevermore, through dust and darkest ash."

Fat tears rolled down my cheeks, sizzling over my red-hot skin. Fear fisted my heart, making me wince in pain.

It wasn't my lips that spoke the last verse of the poem.

It was a man's voice. No, not a man. The timbre was too guttural and hellish to be anything human.

"You mock me, Adaline. For making me wait this long, torturing me with your absence...Now you recite my vow like no time has passed at all."

The old stockade creaked as my body began to shake involuntarily.

Run, a voice in my head screamed. *Danger.*

But I couldn't move an inch. I was trapped. I couldn't even turn my head to glance behind me. Even if I could, I wasn't sure if I would. Something big and terrifying was behind me.

The chance that this was still all a dream was the only thing keeping me from totally losing my mind.

"I–I'm not Adaline Moore. I mean, I am. B–but—"

"Silence!" the voice boomed, his command lashing over my body like a whip, leaving my skin stinging.

"N–no! You have to listen to me!" God, what was I doing? Even in a situation like this—impossible as it was—where it was wise to keep my mouth shut, I couldn't. "I'm not who you're after! S–so don't fucking touch me!"

The energy in the air crackled with electricity like a storm about to break. I didn't need to see behind me to feel the space between us shrink. It stood so close now that its warmth bled into my bare flesh.

The flames behind the entity cast their shadow on the ground in front of me. My heart practically stopped in my chest when I registered the outline of a man's torso. His shoulders and chest were insanely broad, tapering into a trim waist. Anything below hip level was obstructed by my own shadow.

But what was very obvious was exactly what I'd been fearing...And there was another darker part of me that had also hoped for it.

The shadow had a normal, human torso, as far as I could tell. But between his shoulders was something round.

The missing jack-o'-lantern.

"Adaline." My name in the monster's mouth was tender this time, making my breath catch. "I've been waiting for your return. My master swore he'd plant your soul somewhere in your bloodline. The last Moore woman who came to me was docile, delicate. She hadn't a mouth like yours..."

Long, knobby fingers tipped with claws gripped the stockades on either side of my head. Then he arched over me, so his breath tickled my ear and the flames filling his eye sockets licked my temple.

Just like the rest of the fire, it didn't hurt. It felt...*good*.

"So, how could you be anyone other than my sweet Adaline?"

I slowly turned my head. He arched over me far enough that I could see most of his pumpkin face. I tried to breathe, but I couldn't.

It was him. It was really him.

Jack Calloway.

Or whatever the devil left of him.

The pumpkin's face was carved with that creepy grin, with thick teeth and mean eyes. Flames danced from those eyes, his mouth, and off the sides—charring nothing.

The thing was, my fear was ebbing away by the second. I looked past his wide grin, deep into the crackling flames.

Something inside that I hadn't known was there ignited.

I swallowed thickly. "I don't remember you."

"In death, I've forgotten much of you as well." His tone dropped to a whisper so terrifyingly wondrous, like the rustle of a thousand dead leaves. "All I remember is that you belong to me, witch."

CHAPTER 6
JACK

She was so responsive to me, and I hadn't even touched her yet.

I'd waited so long, I ached to taste her delicious, supple body. To slide my tongue over her pliable skin. To see her flesh puff and pinken in response to the rough manner in which she'd always begged me to take her.

But I held my ground, battling the dark urges to claim my witch while she was bound up so sweetly for me in the stockades.

Like an offering.

So long I'd spent in Hell. So *fucking* long. How many decades had it been? How many centuries? It hurt to think about. Not because the concept of time was difficult for the dead but because it filled me with an infernal rage to dwell on what we'd lost.

The years we could have had together. The life.

They'd ripped it away from us in the cruelest way conceivable.

Now it was all...*twisted*.

We'd been reunited by the darkest of magic. Magic that came with a high price tag. But along with our old physical appearances, our memories were gone, too.

Still, I'd never forget how much my entire being ached for my beloved witch.

I had to have her. All of her.

Her sweat. Her blood. Her tears. Her come.

I'd savor every drop as I devoured her.

Then I'd reclaim her soul so that I might spend eternity with Adaline.

But I wouldn't have her hating me. When she shook, it would be in ecstasy, not fear. So when she shrieked for me not to touch her, I obeyed.

I wanted her to crave me. Very soon, I'd have her begging for my touch.

How long had it been since a Moore came to me? I'd made a mistake, thinking the last one carried my Adaline's soul. I'd terrified the poor woman. I barely even touched her, and she broke.

The Moore to carry my beloved's soul wouldn't be so fragile.

If I was wrong about this one, and this woman wasn't carrying my beloved's soul either, she could meet the same fate as the last.

I directed my attention back to the girl's scent, taking her aroma deep into my lungs. She smelled of dark and dormant magic. Of flame and misfortune. Of unholy miracles rooted deep in her bones.

But they'd all smelled like that. I'd made a deal with the devil to spare her soul and return it to me so one day I could claim it for myself.

The arrangement came with strings attached. Strings so heavy, they were more like chains. I'd become a monster. A bedtime story to scare children.

The worst part was never knowing when she'd come back or if I'd missed her completely.

They never came to the hill. They were afraid. Especially after I'd frightened the last one half to death.

I needed a taste to know it was her. Memories had faded, but I'd never forget Adaline's taste. It didn't matter if her body was new or if her thoughts of me had long faded from her mind. She'd still taste like those stolen nights. The vow I'd made to her that night in the woods had been drawn upon her flesh, sealed with ancient magic. I was bound to her blood, her flesh, her *soul*.

One taste and I'd know.

She quivered against me, her flesh brushing against mine. *Heretics and hellfire.* She was so soft. So beautiful. My fire had consumed her clothing, leaving her body bare for me. Her skin was snow white, with a light smattering of freckles. Her curves were sinful and pure all at once.

This new body of hers was virginal, too, judging by the scent.

I leaned closer, bringing my face to her hair and inhaling. Oh, to have her tight little cunt wrapped around my cock. To feel the throb of her heartbeat, stroking me from the inside as I took her virginity for the second time. My dark and lusty thoughts turned as black as pitch when I noticed the mark on her cheek. Her flesh was red and inflamed.

I was in control of this land on All Hallows' Eve, so my flames wouldn't hurt her. But the inflammation wasn't a burn.

It was a handprint. A man's.

Someone had struck her and left her here to die in the fire.

Painful memories stirred.

I released a roar, and the flames engulfing my head blazed white hot. Ada's eyes grew wide, my monstrous face grinning back at me through their reflection.

"Who did this to you? Who touched what's mine?"

CHAPTER 7
ADA

J ack's rage shook the night and split my ears.

But I wasn't afraid. Which was totally nuts. I should have been. There was a monster right behind me, looming over me with flames rolling off his pumpkin head. A freaking *pumpkin* head!

By now, all my fear had crumbled to ash. I wasn't sure why. Maybe because shock was setting in. Or I was still holding out hope that this was just a dream and I'd snap awake any minute now.

There was also the slightest chance that this was happening. That this was real, that Jack Calloway was possessing the Jack-o'-lantern and that I really was the reincarnated soul of my ancestor…And that I was just locked up in the stockades, conveniently naked and unable to run away.

I mean, what were the odds?

Goosebumps exploded over my skin when a problematic thought unfurled. I wanted this to be real.

I wanted to be this monster's woman.

I wanted him to kill Lucas Reed for daring to lay a hand on me.

How fucked was that? Then again, that was just being a Moore. We were all twisted, sexually liberated masochists who were long overdue for a little justice. So when the opportunity rolled around in the form of a flaming pumpkin man, how could I say no?

As the seconds passed, my resolve crumbled. "I..."

Jack lifted one of his hands, moving to caress my inflamed cheek, but paused with his sharp nails barely grazing my skin. His desire to touch me was so palpable it made the air tense and suffocating even more than the smoke and fire.

"Tell me who hurt you, little one. I'll spill their blood and send their soul to Satan in your honor. I'll rip out his heart and give it to you, my heart's flame."

Heart's flame.

I opened my mouth, but before anything came out, the cornstalks on the edge of the pumpkin patch rustled. I wouldn't have noticed in the wake of the burning pumpkin patch if it wasn't for Jack's head snapping in the movement's direction.

I saw him a breath later.

Lucas.

I could see his shitty Freddy Krueger makeup—which was half melted from the heat of the fire—through the cornstalks. Then I picked out the other sets of eyes gawking at us, their faces white as a sheet. About half the group must have gotten the nerve to venture back.

Why? Why had they come back?

To set me free? No...If they gave two gummy rat shits about me, they would never have left me in the first place.

Once they realized they'd been spotted, they took off running.

Jack pushed off from where he was arched over me in the stockades and strode around, bringing himself to stand in front of me.

My stomach fluttered as I took in the sight of his body.

He was tall, at least seven if not eight feet. His shoulders were broad, just like his shadow betrayed, and his arms were long, muscular, and threaded with bulging veins that made my mouth water. He was completely ripped, with bulging pectorals and tightly defined abs. The finest dusting of hair stretched from his navel and disappeared into his pants, which sat low on his hips. They were black, tight-fitting breeches, ones typical for men from the late seventeenth century. The laces were stretched just a little too tight in order to hold his manhood.

Catching me ogling him, the monster cackled. The flames in his triangular eye sockets jumped with the rhythm of his husky laughter. "Look how my witch's hunger grows. The question is, what does she crave more? Vengeance or my cock?"

Neither! my morality screamed in my ear.

Both, something darker whispered in the other.

Seemingly reading my mind, the corners of the monster's carved grin widened. Then he raised his arms at his sides, palms up, and with another cackle that rolled from some place deep in his chest, the ground rumbled. A second later, pumpkin vines shot up from the earth in a spray of soil.

The vines sailed through the air, into the cornfield, and probed around for several of the longest seconds of my life. Then there was a rustle of the stalks, and the distressed sounds of my classmates shattered the silence. A few breaths later, six of Jack's vines came back with captives.

He lifted them over the smaller fires that still burned and kept them hoisted in the air for me to see, each of their heads dangling a few inches off the ground.

There was Chelsea, Derrick, the three boys who'd manhandled me in the cornfield earlier that night, and Lucas.

Most of them were too terrified to say anything, with their eyes averted to the ground, refusing to look at me. Lucas was the only one who looked straight at me. Not in the eye, of course. He was too busy wolfing up the sight of my naked body, bent over in the stockades.

Jack seemed to notice the shameless way the biggest of the young men stared at me. Another vine coiled around Luc's throat. His eyes bulged as his captor slowly cut his air supply.

"*You*," Jack growled. "You dare look at what's mine?" He bounced the vine entwined around Luc's ankle, making him bob like a pinata. "Is he the one who struck you, my flame?"

I hesitated. If I said yes, this would be the end of the road for Lucas Reed.

He deserved to die.

But...it was still murder. Then again, if he was dead, there'd be no chance of him hurting me again. There'd be no chance of him hurting any woman in the way he'd tried to hurt me.

The second pause was all Lucas needed. He swung his Freddy Kruger claw up and swiped it over the vines curled around his throat.

Jack snarled and, in his surprise, dropped Luc, who scurried away like a cockroach, making a beeline for something to hide and cower beneath.

"It's alright. Let him go. I have a feeling he'll be back."

All five captives scrunched their faces, probably thinking I was insane. Because who in their right mind would come back to the scene of his near death, especially when his would-be murderer was a pumpkin-headed ghost monster with command over earth and fire?

Lucas. That's who. Now that he knew Jack Calloway's ghost actually existed, there was no doubt the drunk would come crawling back to watch me get torn apart. He was a sick bastard like that. Sicker than me. Which was saying something because I was the chick developing a crush on the pumpkin-headed boogeyman of Hallow Hill.

"Let those two go." I flexed a finger, pointing to Chelsea and Derrick. "They're good."

I wasn't about to give these two a pass for basically being Switzerland between Luc and me. But they didn't deserve to die. Chelsea always did her best to stick up for me. Her best sucked, but you had to give the girl an A for effort. As for Derrick, if it wasn't for his interception earlier... My stomach flipped just thinking about it.

Jack released the couple. They fell to the ground and, without looking back, scrambled into the night.

"Wha–what about us, Ada?" one of my attackers stammered. "Lucas was the one that wanted you to come here tonight in the first place. He was the one who had us throw you in the stocks. He wanted to see you get fucked by Pumpkin Head. Not us!"

"Yeah! We were just having a bit of fun earlier."

My gaze hardened, and my tummy went tense. I waited for remorse to set in. It didn't.

Whatever humanity had me hesitating earlier with Lucas withered and died inside me. The thing was, I didn't have to say anything to seal their fate. Their crappy attempt to save their asses had the opposite effect.

Jack lifted the vines, bringing all of them close to his flame-filled grin.

He radiated violence, with a menacing grin that could live forever in your nightmares and an aura made of literal fire.

This was a monster.

Ready to kill.

They all cowered and whimpered as they dangled helplessly from Jack's vines, their faces stained beet-red from all the blood draining into their heads. One guy pissed himself, his costume leg turning dark with pungent liquid. It was ironic since he was dressed as the devil.

Still, no sympathy stirred. I was too jaded from all the years of torment. Plus, I was a Moore female. We didn't have much sympathy for the trash in this town who saw our spark of light inside and tried to stomp it out. I had generations of bitterness clogging my veins, causing my heart to run black.

The only emotion that ignited was satisfaction when Jack's rough timbre turned demonic and booming. "You've barely reached manhood. You're too young to die. But your hands carry the scent of my woman. *My* mate!"

"W–we were just playing a–a–a g–game," one of the guys stammered. This one hadn't wet himself, but he looked like he was on the verge of vomiting.

Jack's pumpkin head swiveled in my direction. "What kind of game?"

Damn. This vengeful spirit was so furious I could practically taste his ire lacing the night air. But he was still giving them a fair trial.

I could lie. Would Jack know? It made me wonder if he'd let them go even if he knew what they'd nearly done earlier tonight.

I decided I didn't care enough to find out.

"Game?" I pushed out a bitter laugh. "Funny. Most people just call it attempted rape."

The flames filling Jack's head died for a moment. When they ignited a few seconds later, they came back as a pale and sinister hue of blue.

A dark thrill shot through me at the prospect of seeing Jack avenge me.

My blood boiled with hatred, and nothing but sinister satisfaction wound through me as more of Jack's vines wiggled around their master's victims and began to squeeze.

They sputtered and choked, and all I could do was watch as the life was slowly strangled from them.

They may have never gotten what they were after tonight, but a part of me somehow knew they would have eventually. Lucas would have claimed me first and then probably thrown them whatever scraps were left of me once he had finished.

So...I felt nothing but cold relief when they fell limp one by one in short succession, the light gone from their eyes.

They were dead.

Gone.

Nothing but corpses in costumes.

Jack threw their bodies into the fire that had spread to the perimeter of the pumpkin patch.

With a shake of his head, he pivoted to face me fully once again. His grin was faint, but it was still there. It was always there. "Frightened of me now, witch?"

I shook my head. "No. I should be. But I'm not."

"I just murdered three children."

"They were all eighteen." I shrugged. "Actually, two of them were nineteen. They were so dumb they got held back a year. You did it for me, to keep me safe. That doesn't scare me."

Brief silence flickered between us as Jack stared me down, causing me to squirm in the stockade.

His flames turned back to orange, a crackling hum rumbling from his chest. "As much as I enjoy seeing you bent over like that, it can't be comfortable."

My heart rate spiked. Was he offering to set me free? I mean, he literally just killed for me. So why wouldn't he want me to be free? A monster like him was supposed to take advantage of me and fuck me with whatever he had hidden in those breeches.

Jesus. What was wrong with me? I just watched three people I'd known since childhood die.

I should have felt something that wasn't...this.

I wasn't really sure what "this" was, but it bled into my

bloodstream, siphoned to my heart, and exploded inside my chest like a hundred firecrackers going off at once.

My hands clenched into shaking fists beside my head. "Maybe I should stay locked here. I was the one who wanted them to die. You were just protecting me."

I was the one who wanted them to suffer.

"Don't feel remorse. They don't deserve it. Only worthless men put their hands on a woman without her permission. So you don't owe them pity."

He was right. They didn't deserve my pity. They might have been dressed up as monsters, but the costumes hadn't fooled me. Behind the rubber masks were real-life monsters.

Jack took a step closer, the air growing hotter as the distance between us shrunk. "But I think you're right. I think you should stay locked up. Just for a little longer."

I gulped, throat bobbing. "Wh–why?"

"I think you know why. You want to see what I'll do to you while you're bent over like that, naked and helpless. Don't you, Adaline?"

"I... I do," I admitted.

He took another step, then another, until he was directly in front of me. Then he crouched so we were face to face. His pumpkin head was so close that if he had a nose, it would be touching mine.

"I'm going to keep my hands off you because that's what you told me to do," he said in a softer tone that filled me with a warm fuzzy feeling.

"I won't touch you until you *beg* me to do so, witch."

And just like that, the pleasant warmth pooling in my lower stomach turned to lava, making me melt.

His vines aimed at me, and I gasped when one spiraled around my ankle and up my leg.

"But I will pleasure you, Ada. I'll make you come. Then I'll release you from the stocks." His manic grin stretched wider, crackling ominously. "On one condition."

"What's that?" I gasped, moaning as the vine's blunted tip teased the seam of my center. It was surprisingly smooth.

Jack smirked. "Scream for me."

CHAPTER 8
ADA

A fluttering feeling swept over my apex. My pussy was already so wet, even though the vines dancing over my body had barely begun.

One tendril curled around my breast and flicked at my nipple. Another wrapped around my waist, echoing the possessiveness in Jack's demeanor.

This reminded me of a tentacle porno I'd seen once. Only without the seventeenth-century heartthrob who pledged himself to the devil to save his lover and got a pumpkin head and tentacle vines for his trouble.

As Jack's vines teased my lips, my pussy throbbed with need. Being horny wasn't exactly a new thing for me.

I was a virgin, but I wasn't a saint.

I mean, I was an eighteen-year-old with an internet connection. I'd bought myself a vibrator on my birthday, and Lord, it had seen some action since. So I was no stranger to orgasms. But this wasn't even in the same universe as far as my sexual experiences went. I was way out of my depth. I'd graduated from girls' first vibrator to hardcore monster peen.

The lust filling my veins, making me sweat and squirm, was too much to focus on anything else. I was so lost in my need for friction that all my inhibitions got lost in the haze and smoke.

For a moment, I allowed myself to believe Jack Calloway was real and that he was mine.

When the vine slipped through my folds to rub teasing circles around my clit I released a soft "*Oh.*"

I roved my hips, trying to get it to apply pressure to the place it kept dancing around. "P–please."

Jack laughed, changing up the movement of the vine so it painted long strokes over my seam, touching every inch of my sensitive skin from my clit, over my opening, to the tight ring of flesh behind. Every time it passed over a hole, I tensed, preparing for penetration.

I moaned loudly as he drove me closer to that promise of release. "P–please," I said again as I squeezed my thighs together, trying to trap the vine as it passed over my entrance.

I yelped when it pulled back and lashed over my ass cheek.

Jack angled his pumpkin head as he prowled closer. "You're going to have to do better than that. You want to be filled by the only male capable of fucking you without getting burned?"

I gave a frantic nod. The vine's rounded head sunk into me on the next gasping breath.

Jack's flames burned brighter with his smile. "That's a good little witch. Take it. Take all I have to give you."

Another vine wrapped around my thigh, biting into my skin just enough to be pleasurable, and spread my stance wider. He went so slow. He had to know this was my first time because he was excruciatingly gentle.

I got lost in the fire in Jack's eyes as he eased me into madness.

Jack watched me intently, that permanent smirk affixed to his face as the pumpkin vine slipped deeper inside me, working me so slowly it was almost painful. I bore down on it, trying to force more of its length inside me. "More. Give me more."

"Such a lusty little thing," he said with a grating chuckle, flames flickering at the sound. "So insatiable."

As he laughed, his muscles flexed, and his sweat-streaked skin gleamed in the ominous glow of the firelight.

I wanted to touch him. To explore his strangely exotic body, to trace every bulging vein and slab of muscle with my tongue. I got wetter with the thought of it.

"Oh, Jack."

He stilled, the invading appendage freezing inside me.

"Why did you stop?"

His gaze flickered as he gave a sharp exhale. "Say it again. Say my name." He resumed stroking me from the inside, the vine picking up its pace.

"*Jack.*"

He leaned forward and braced a hand on the wooden frame of the stockade as if hearing his name in my mouth was some kind of spiritual experience. "Oh. Fuck. *Ada.*"

There was so much affection brimming in his hellish voice.

This was real. This really was the ghost of Jack Calloway, and he was totally convinced that I held the soul of his lover. What would he do if he decided I wasn't?

I wasn't expecting a four-hundred-year-old pumpkin-headed ghost monster, but I knew it was a bad idea fucking one. Especially when it thought you were someone else.

I was playing with fire. Literally.

Still...I couldn't bring myself to care enough to stop this. I was drunk with lust. My inhibitions must have burned in the fire like my clothes.

I needed to see this through. Something bigger than anything I'd ever felt before was pushing for me to throw myself in the fire so I could see what came from the ashes.

My walls tightened and clenched around the vine and—oh God. A second tendril slithered inside to join the first, stretching me, both vines thrusting at alternating depths, one in, one out. Faster, deeper. Plunging inside at a pace that had turned punishing.

Fuck.

It was good.

Almost too good.

I cried out, gasping down gulps of hot air in hopes of a reprieve for my burning lungs.

My eyes drifted shut as I braced myself for the waves of my incoming climax.

"Keep your eyes on me," Jack commanded, his hand clutching the slab of wood near my head hard enough to make it crack.

I wasn't one for obeying orders. Especially when they came from a guy. But Jack was different. This was a monster, one whose vines had rooted themselves inside me and ran my heart through on their path to retrieve my soul.

Here I was in the middle of a pumpkin patch, buck ass naked, locked in medieval fucking stockades with a very aroused man with a jack-o'-lantern head, fucking my brains out with his magical pumpkin vines.

And I was eating up every damn thing he gave me.

So I obeyed, staring into his ember-filled gaze. Completely mesmerized.

"That's it," he crooned. "Are you going to be a good little witch and scream for me?"

He brought a third pumpkin vine to my center, grinding it against my clit.

Christ. He was applying the perfect amount of pressure.

I screamed with my release, the sound turning to whimpers as he praised me with a soft, "*Good* girl."

I screamed again when it curled inside me to hit a spot that had me seeing stars.

My legs turned to jelly, making me almost grateful for the stockade propping me up.

Jack released a purring laugh that had his flames burning white, then back to orange. The heat of his face warmed my own.

When he pulled the pumpkin vine from me—with an embarrassing wet noise—I cried out at the loss.

The vine rose so that it was in front of my face. It was covered in so much of my juices that it dripped down its dark green skin. "Look at how needy you are, my heart's flame. I wonder how you taste?"

A long, meaty tongue slid from the pumpkin's mouth and coiled around the vine. It was so long that it circled it a few times. Then he pulled his tongue back into his mouth and released a deep, pleasure-laced hum.

Like it was the best thing he'd ever put in his mouth.

"What do I taste like?" Curiosity had the question tumbling from my lips before I could hold it back.

A deep and satisfied growl echoed from his chest. "Exactly how I remember."

CHAPTER 9
JACK

My witch tasted like dark magic and sin. I'd forgotten so much from our past life, but I'd never forget the taste of her forbidden fruit.

It was her. I was damn sure before, but her taste confirmed it. This was the Moore female who carried my witch's soul.

Gods. I ached to claim her mouth. Her pert lips were so plush, so perfectly fuckable.

I cupped her cheek, my thumb stroking her soft skin. Her flame-orange lashes fluttered, knocking the tears beaded there loose.

Hellfire and heretics. She was so damn beautiful.

"You burn so brightly for me, my heart's flame."

Her tear-filled eyes widened at my words. Her body still tremored as the last waves of her orgasm washed over her. "Jack..."

My cock throbbed from hearing my name in her mouth again.

"Please. Touch me."

Finally. It was agony holding back. I wanted nothing more than to free my hunger and take her right here in the stockades.

I fought back the dark voice in my head, urging me to claim

her hard and fast. I'd waited too long for this night to have it be over so soon.

I'd draw this out.

By the time I was ready to feed her my cock, I'd have her writhing, *screaming* for it.

Pressing a finger under her chin, I lifted her head, so her eyes locked with mine. I had no lips to kiss her with, so I granted her my tongue, making a show of it.

Her little heartbeat fluttered as she watched the way my tongue slowly snaked from my carved mouth. It was thick, slimy, and looked more like a tentacle than a tongue.

Her eyes stretched so wide I thought the monstrous appendage might have scared her. A moment later, that worry was put to the grave when the scent of her arousal filled the air.

Her eyelids grew heavy with lust, and she wet her lips. "Jack, please," she said again. "Touch me."

I released a chuckle that was as soft as her adorable pleas. My tongue glazed over her lips, then prodded at her mouth. Like a good girl, she opened for me.

My tongue swirled around hers, tickling and twirling, then switching up its movement and sliding and stroking over every inch of skin, leaving nothing untouched. I wanted to give her an idea of what this part of me could do. How I could please her without laying a single finger on her body.

The kiss was obscene, noisy, and frantic.

I held her mouth prisoner until she was shaking with the need for oxygen. Her chest heaved violently, and I gave a squeeze of her breasts with my vines that were still coiled tightly around them. With the pumpkin vines, it wasn't the same as touching her.

I couldn't feel her skin, but I could still enjoy the sight of her soft mounds staining vibrant shades of pink and red as I slowly cut off the blood flow from them. Slowly, I applied more pressure—carefully observing her to ensure I didn't do any actual damage.

"Does it hurt, little witch?"

"Y–yes. But—fuck. It's g–good. It hurts so good. I want more."

"Tell me exactly what you want, witch, and I just might indulge you."

"I want you to touch me."

"You said that. Be specific."

"With your tongue..."

I leaned back, my vines unwinding from her breasts and dropping to the ground. She gave a frustrated little huff when I stopped touching her completely.

"Beg me for it."

"Please."

"You call that begging? You're going to have to do better than that, witch."

That little spark of defiance I loved so much lit up her eyes. She fought against her stocks, making the old wood groan. "Jack! Please! I need you to touch me." She sucked in a breath, and when she spoke again, her voice was an electric-charged whisper. "I *need* it."

I understood her urgency.

This was more than just lust and adrenaline driving us toward one another.

This was something darker at play. Something the devil himself had a hand in orchestrating.

A pleased growl purred from my throat. I told her I'd free her from the stockade if she was a good little witch and screamed for me. She'd done just that. But I knew by the mouth-watering scent of her arousal that she wasn't ready to be set loose just yet.

For her, I needed to treasure her. To fulfill her every whim and need in a way this worthless town could never fulfill.

For me, she needed to sate an ancient hunger only she could.

I strode behind her and collapsed to my knees as if in prayer and brought my face level with her opening.

They'd always said I worshipped the devil.

But no. It was her I worshipped.

I smoothed my hand over the subtle curve of her rear, touching her for the first time. Her body hitched against my palm, and a tiny "oh," tumbled from her.

Gripping her thighs, I spread her legs wide apart and slathered a long lick over her dripping cunt.

I couldn't put words to how damn good she tasted. Like Heaven. Like Hell. Like eternal damnation and salvation at the same time.

I didn't have the willpower to tease this out as I did with the vines. With her flavor soaking my tongue, I was going feral for more. I couldn't wait a second longer.

I'd already waited an eternity to feel her heat around me.

I plunged my tongue into her core and groaned into her when her body jerked in surprise.

Her heartbeat pattered against my tongue through her quivering walls. I licked every inch of her insides, leaving nothing claimed.

The wooden stockade that propped her up rattled as she tried to turn her head so she could see what I was doing to her and huffed when she couldn't.

I knew I'd track down the human that had placed her here before the night was out and tear his heart out for his crimes. For now, we were both enjoying the dark little game the stocks presented.

We still reveled in one another in ways so devious that our

playtimes had literally gone down in history. There were some things time could never change.

Ada thrashed as I licked and lavished her core, plunging in and out with a frantic pace that had her screaming again.

Deeper, I thrust, occasionally pulling out to tease her clit before sinking back into her heat.

She came again, coating my tongue in her sweetness. My fingers bit into her thighs to hold her steady as she rode through the waves of bliss.

Her chest heaved. Her sweat-soaked flesh blotted with pink splotches brought on by the pleasure, and her head sagged in the stocks.

She was tired. Too bad I wasn't even close to being through with her.

This was just the beginning.

I reached for the padlock, keeping her locked inside the crude device, and snapped it off with a jerk of my wrist. Then I ripped the wooden slat over her head, clean off its hinges, and tossed it away.

She was free.

Stretching to her full height, her eye level barely came to the top ridge of my abs. So small. Easy to break if I wasn't careful.

"Wh–what now?" she asked.

I bent toward her so suddenly she stumbled, tripped over the stockade's broken piece and landed on her rear.

Looming over her, I laughed.

"Now I make you pay for all those years you made me wait. All those All Hallows' Eves, where you never came for me. So crawl away as fast as you can through my pumpkin patch, little field mouse. I'll still catch you."

My hand dropped to clutch my rock-hard bulge, straining against my breeches. "And when I do, I'm going to break you open and claim your soul...and whatever else spills out."

CHAPTER 10
ADA

I sprinted through the flaming pumpkin patch with my heart pounding wildly in my throat.

The fire still burned through the pumpkin patch, but the pumpkins remained unscorched. The only thing his flames had eaten was my clothes—except for my shoes. My black-and-white checkered Vans were singed but mostly intact.

Their rubber soles slapped against the ground, kicking up soil as I ran faster than I ever had before.

Why was I running so hard? I wanted him to catch me.

I'd had a small taste of what his vines could do. And that *tongue*...Holy Hell. My whole body throbbed at the very fresh memory of how his tongue had danced over my lips, filled my mouth, curled inside me.

This entire night was crazy. If this was a dream, I didn't want it to end.

And if it wasn't...? Well...things couldn't go back to the way they were. People died tonight. Even if shit went back to normal, how could I go back to school and just pretend that none of this happened?

It would be impossible. I couldn't just forget that my classmates—the ones who'd survived—had left me for dead.

I couldn't just pretend I hadn't fallen for the monster in my favorite bedtime story.

Maybe that's why I was running.

I wanted him to chase me. I wanted him to be so damn ravenous by the time he caught me that he'd make good on all his dark promises.

Whether or not I carried the soul of the original Adaline Moore, I didn't care. I was hooked on the fantasy that I belonged with him.

Because I was so damn desperate to find a place I belonged.

Maybe that place was in the arms of Jack Calloway.

I had no idea what kind of cock a creature like him possessed. Would it be human? Doubtful. One thing was for sure, it was going to be bigger than the average male member. With curiosity practically eating me alive, I threw a glance over my shoulder to see how close the monster was.

I shouldn't have looked.

My foot caught on a pumpkin, and I went sailing face-first into the dirt. As soon as my hands and knees made contact with the ground, pumpkin stalks, just like the one that had gotten me off, lurched up from the dirt and captured my wrists and ankles.

I cried out in shock as they hoisted me into the air and flipped me around until my back hovered several feet off the ground, belly up. The vines stretched my limbs taut.

I felt like a tiny bug caught in a spider's web. Totally helpless. About to be something else's meal.

So why was my pulse roaring in my ears? Not in fear. In excitement.

I wanted to be eaten.

Jack stepped through a wall of flames, looking like a demon from Hell as smoke writhed around his legs. My breath quickened when he loomed over me, cocking his pumpkin head while his carved grin turned sadistic.

"Caught you," he said with a low growl.

The sexual tension couldn't be any thicker.

"Let you," I breathed.

"Then you're a foolish little thing. Like a moth to a flame, flocking to your own destruction."

My sex pulsed at the inflection in his voice, rough with hunger and full of ache. "I'm not afraid of you."

Every muscle in my body clenched as he prowled closer until he stood between my spread legs. He reached out with his huge hand and cupped my center possessively. "You should be. Look what's come from loving me. A centuries-old curse that has plagued your whole family. Now that we're together again, I'm not the same. I'm twisted by dark magic."

My blood turned hot, practically singing through my veins. "I don't care. I want you."

"Say it again." His digits threaded through the curls of my pubic hair—the reverence of his fingers catching me off guard.

How could a terrifying monster like him be so...tender?

"I want you, Jack. I fucking want you so bad it hurts."

Like the shift of the breeze, his demeanor turned on a dime.

He muttered something in a demonic language, and the vines loosened a beat later, lowering me to his hip level. With one hand, he cupped my ass and palmed my pliant flesh, wincing with his suddenly bruising grip, tugging me closer. His other hand rubbed over my seam, his ministrations gentle but firm as he spread my juices around.

"You're not yet ready for me," he said. "If I take you now, I'll break you in half."

I shivered in dark delight. "Break me then."

"Your eagerness for me is pleasing. After all this time, when wicked magic has twisted my appearance, you still want me.

You are truly mine. My brazen little witch. How I've missed your flame. Your body." He bowed his spine and draped his torso over mine, so his fiery eyes filled my vision as two of his fingers filled my pussy.

Rather than pumping his fingers in and out with the motion of his arm, the hand cupping my ass rocked me, slow at first and building momentum. I swung on the vines, back and forth, gravity doing most of the work as I was lifted off his digits, then came back down, gasping every time our bodies met.

The rhythm of it was insanely perfect. My nerves lit up with the way Jack filled me, how he was pleasuring me in a way that drew on my every sense. The warmth of the fire., the breeze blowing through my hair as I sailed through the air… His rich scent of earth and smoke filled my nostrils every time I swung back down.

The taste of the dark magic making this all possible sat heavy on my tongue, my walls clenching around him every time his fingers speared me as if trying to keep him inside just a little longer.

"Your cunt's so slick for me…" His tongue slithered from his gaping mouth and licked a path from my navel to my breasts. "Memories are coming back, Ada. Seeing you spread for me like this is allowing me to remember. The way sweat pearls on your skin. The sweet scent of your arousal. The way your buds pucker like cherries when I do this…" The tip of his tongue laved around my nipples, slurping at them noisily. He drew back, the tentacle-like appendage disappearing back into his head.

He emitted a grave-deep chuckle. "I remember how you always struggled to be quiet when I fucked you in the woods. We feared the village would discover the depths of our wickedness, so I'd often have to gag you by stuffing your undergarments into your mouth."

His voice dropped to a serpentine whisper. "You always got so wet when I did that."

When I swung back down, he hooked an arm under my thigh and held me still, locking me in place around him. "Now, you can scream as loud as you want. But if this will make you wetter, you might just be able to take my cock."

Another vine crept over my shoulder and slowly snaked around my head to cover my mouth completely. He took a step back and laughed when I tried to wiggle closer to reclaim the missing heat of him.

When his hand dropped to pull at the laces of his breeches, I realized he'd positioned himself so that I could see exactly what I was about to get fucked with.

When he worked the laces through the last rivet, he wrenched his breeches down and freed his hunger. Fisting his base, he grinned sadistically as I took in the monstrosity between his thighs with wide eyes. It was a light brown, almost green color. The shaft started off thick, then tapered off and curved slightly upward—like the stem of the largest pumpkin known to man.

I began to shake with anticipation. It wasn't that I was scared of taking him, like any other person in my place would be. This town had turned me into such a distrustful person. I didn't trust a single goddamn human alive.

But I trusted this monster with everything. My life. My body. My soul.

And it felt so goddamn right.

"Look at you. All bound up. So wet and needy, ready for your monster to crawl from Hell's flames and fuck you. Is that what you want, Ada? For me to take you?"

A swollen moan bled from me, muffled by the vines covering my mouth.

Jack smirked. "I'll take that as a yes."

The next thing I knew, the vines were flipping me over and lowering me into a kneeling position on the ground.

The vines twisted my arms into a folded position behind my back and spread my legs wide while keeping my ankles pinned.

The ground shook as Jack knelt behind me. He gripped the back of my neck and gently bent me forward until the cool soil met the warm flesh of my cheek.

He's going to take me from behind.

The position reminded me of the sultry bondage videos I'd seen online, where the woman was bound with red silk rope and placed in precarious positions. Shibari, I think it was called.

I could barely move. And that somehow made me all the wetter.

Gripping the flesh of my hips with one hand, Jack pulled himself flush against me. My breath hitched. There was so much promise in the warmth caressing my core.

The dead, the ghosts, whatever dark entities watched us this night had to be clutching their goddamn pearls at the sight of me on my knees, face first in the earth, gagged and bound with a pumpkin-headed monster about to take my virginity.

I almost didn't blame Lucas for wanting to see this.

I'd never felt so wickedly beautiful.

I wiggled my hips, trying to entice Jack to penetrate me because he was taking his goddamn time. All I got was a cruel laugh feathering over my backside.

"Look at my witch squirm. So small and delicate, so eager to be broken."

Fuck me. His voice was so dark and guttural, it crawled up my spine and wrapped around my throat, locking me in a chokehold I knew would last long after this moment.

I'd never been *this* aroused before. The euphoria flooding through me was so overwhelming my head swam.

"You know I'm about to claim much more than your cunt,

right, Adaline? The cost of bringing us together again was great. Don't be fool enough to think I was the only one to pay the price. Once I claim you, there's no turning back to your normal human life."

No turning back. My mind blanched. Where there should have been a pang of fear, or at least second thoughts, there was none. I didn't have to think about it. There was no question in my mind about what I needed to do because I barely had a life here, so there was no point in even considering choosing my life over Jack.

I had no life here. It was miserably boring, so suffocating I wanted to scream. And the worst part was that it was lonely.

This was the opposite of that. For the first time, I felt alive, hot and bright, like a flame that had had its oxygen cut for so long, it forgot it had ever burned.

Jack's hand gripped my hip possessively while he canted his own, sliding his throbbing cock through my slick folds. "Last chance to change your mind, witch."

He loosened the vines just enough so I could speak. I angled my head, peering back at him over my shoulder.

"I choose you."

CHAPTER II
ADA

"When they burned you at the stake, they thought they were sending you to Hell." Jack's grip turned bruising on my flesh, knocking a lusty mewl from my mouth. He laughed, deep and guttural, making tongues of fire explode from his carved facial features. "But you, little witch, must step through the black gates of your own accord."

My heart sped up as he paused with the head of his cock sliding through my folds a few times before lining himself up with his hips drawn back—ready to fill me.

But he didn't. He was giving me yet another out.

"Jack. Fuck me, damn it."

Before the sentence had fully left my mouth, he pushed his length into me with a swift jab of his hips. It was manageable at first with the stem-like girth but grew thicker the more he fed me.

My muscles spasmed in ecstasy. It was heaven and hell all at the same time. Painful bliss and delicious torment. "Oh, God. *Ahhg!*"

He slapped my ass hard enough for me to see stars. "There's no God here, witch. He forsook both of us long ago. If you wish to scream a name other than mine, cry out to the devil. He's the only one who has looked upon our union and *smiled*."

I trembled as sinful words and acrid smoke wrapped my mind in a disorienting haze.

Jack's primal growl shook my whole world. He arched over me, claws wrapping around my neck—his fingers so large his nails dug into my trachea.

Then—*Jesus Christ*—he began to work himself in and out, making me stretch and take every glorious inch of his stem.

His claws bit into my flesh as he thrust, each stroke more fevered than the last. When he'd said he might break me, he wasn't kidding. His mass was so thick the pain was nearly blinding. But the unique curve of his cock hit that button inside me each time he filled me to the brim. Each of his punishing thrusts morphed the pain into burning pleasure.

I groaned and moaned with every thrust, drooling as the vines cut into my mouth. The sounds were more animal than anything. Then again, with Jack, I felt more like a monster than a human.

This town had spent my whole life demonizing me. It only seemed fitting that I ended up getting railed by one.

My toes curled into the soil. My breathing came out in short, uneven huffs. I wanted him to devour me. To use me. To take me and drag me to hell and back. Or maybe we wouldn't come back at all.

Each time he surged into me, he buried me to the hilt. Then emptiness filled me when he pulled back, and in the next breath, his glorious heat filled me again with another jerk of his hips.

His pace was uneven and desperate, but his ravenous rhythm only made me wetter. My inner walls tightened as Jack bowed forward, running his tongue up my back to trace the ridge of my spine.

My nerves went into overdrive with the ridiculous amount of sensation Jack poured into my body.

I was so close. *So damn close.*

He began thrusting into me so savagely that the slap of flesh on flesh filled the air. I tried to buck my hips so I could meet the piston of his, but his vines and hands continued to hold me down. This was a lot for my first time. And it was perfect.

He was so forceful. So greedy. So monstrous. Yet there was love in his brutality as he pushed me close to the breaking point but kept me teetering on the edge, still careful to keep me safe and whole while tearing me to shreds with the same ministrations that held me safe and close.

Jack reached around me, his finger slipping between my folds to rub my clit in small, tortuous circles. For someone who hadn't had sex in four hundred years, his precision was impressive. Pressing my face into the ground, I screamed my release into the soil.

The vines fell away from my face, and the next thing I knew, Jack had a handful of my hair, wrenching my head back, so my shriek filled the night.

As my body convulsed and twitched, he pounded into me once, twice, three times more. His muscles tightened. He groaned in my ear, flames grazing my flesh and singeing my hair. This time, the flames hurt. But the pain mixed with the bliss just made the climax sinisterly sweet.

A warm explosion of liquid gushed inside. There was so much that I felt it ooze down my thigh and pool in the juncture of my inner knee.

"Such a good little witch. Such a good girl," Jack grunted, his arms wrapped around me and drawing me close as the pumpkin vines uncoiled from me and withdrew back into the dirt.

"And you're all mine, Adaline Moore. Soul and all."

CHAPTER 12
JACK

"Where are we going?" my witch murmured in the most darling voice, so small and sleepy. I looked down at where she was nestled in my arms.

"To a place that's always welcomed us. The woods."

Her freckled cheeks flushed. "And what are you going to do with me there?"

"The same thing I've always done with you in the woods, Adaline."

The pink hue of her cheeks blossomed across the expanse of her skin in a full-body flush. "Ah, so you do remember something of our past life."

"I don't remember," she confessed, lashes batting as she lifted her eyes to mine. "But there are stories about the things you did to her—to me."

"And what do you make of those stories?"

"To the other kids growing up, they were nightmarish. You were the perverted witch who corrupted Adaline Moore."

It was more accurate to say that it was she who'd corrupted me. I didn't remember much from our life before, but I recalled that smile of hers, with all her secrets tucked at the corner of her perfect lips. I remember the first time I saw it. The first time I saw her.

I couldn't recall her face exactly. But those thick orange lashes reigning her soft green eyes were permanently seared in my mind. Then there was her smile, which had me completely spellbound. It had crawled under my skin, rooting its way into my heart, where it remained to this day.

She chewed on her bottom lip. "To me, you were the prince in the story. Cheesy, right?"

If I could have blinked, I would have. "Cheese?"

"Oh. Right. I forgot it's a centuries-old ghost I'm dealing with here." She smiled sheepishly up at me. It was curious how one moment she could be so fierce, her eyes sparking with defiance as she thrashed on my cock. Then she'd be so shy the next. If I remembered right, she only got this way when she was comfortable. Seeing my little flame's vulnerable side was a gift, one that had to be earned.

"As in, silly, I guess. I'm not sure what that meant back in your time."

"Back when I was alive, silly meant 'blissful' or 'happy.' About two centuries later, the meaning changed to 'lacking in reason' or foolish. And the idea of me being a prince is foolish, Adaline."

She sucked a tiny breath through her clenched teeth. "How...How do you know that?"

Oh. So she didn't know...Well. It wasn't too surprising. Her blood was potent and carried the scent of her magic. But her knowledge of witchcraft seemed to have gotten lost somewhere through the ages.

She might have sensed the dark magic in my aura, but I doubt she could discern it enough to know exactly what was twisting my form and keeping me animated.

"I made a deal with the devil. My soul in exchange for saving yours. I belong to Satan now, Adaline."

She reached up, delicate fingers feathering over the smooth flesh of my head. "That's why you look this way?"

Well, fuck me. She wasn't scared. Not even as she slowly picked up on the fact that it wasn't just my physical form that had been warped by the deal I'd struck.

"Yes."

Her heart beat so loud I could practically taste it in my mouth, and her arousal was so strong, it clung to the air around her like perfume. *Fuck.* It took everything in me not to pin her against the nearest tree and bury myself inside her.

"What happens when the sun rises, Jack?"

"The veil between the living and the dead grows thick once more, and I must return to Hell."

"Hell? Do you like it there?"

"I'd like it more if you were there with me."

Her lashes fluttered. "Are you going to take all of me with you or just my soul?"

"I'll take all of you. If that's what you choose."

"I already told you I choose you."

"But now you know what I really am. I am not the prince from your bedtime stories. I am the villain. I am the monster."

"If I go back, I go back to a drunk bitter mother who's let this town snuff out her spark. When I look at her, it's like looking at my future. I see what this town has done to her. *They're* the monsters." My witch took an uneven breath. "I thought leaving town was the answer. I've been hellbent on graduating and getting enough money for a bus ticket out-of-state once I had my diploma in hand. It's why I took the bet to come to the pumpkin patch this night. Now I think that was an excuse to come. Something had been pulling me."

"Your soul is bound to this place. You were waiting to reunite with me."

"If Satan owns you, did you really save my soul? Or did you just delay the inevitable for four hundred years?"

The question caught me by surprise, causing me to stop in my tracks and gape down at her in my arms. "And what's the inevitable, Adaline?"

I knew what she was getting at, and I wanted to hear her say it. I wanted to hear her voice shake when she said—

"That Satan will own me, too."

A barbed silence settled between us. I could feel her skin explode with goosebumps, and her arousal was stronger than ever.

I couldn't hold back a second longer. I had her turned upright and her back pushed against a tree. I groaned, my dick twitching as her legs banded around my waist. "And what if you're right? What if, in my haste to save you, I rushed into a deal with one big fucking loophole. He'd save it. But he'd still own it."

My fingers flexed over her hip where I held her, and I pulled her toward me while simultaneously keeping her pinned against the tree with my weight.

That's what this whole night had been. Push and pull. Between love and monstrous urges. Between Jack Calloway and the sinister entity filling the holes within me that time and dark magic had eaten away.

"Will I end up like this?"

"No." I brought my head closer to hers. Her pupils blew wide as I kept one hand clamped to her hip while raising the other to run the tip of my nail over her lips. "But you will burn, witch."

Her gaze darkened. "Will it hurt?"

"No. Fire can hurt us no more. That was part of the deal. You'll burn like the star you've always been. Bright. Blinding. Brilliant."

"Will I be tortured?" The weight of the question didn't match the rough pitch of her voice. And her arousal was still strong.

That was my Ada. Brave. Daring. Wicked to the core.

Speaking of her core, it was dripping. My grip slipped from her waist and slowly trailed to caress her center. I wedged my large fingers between her thighs.

My grin twitched. "Yes. But I promise you'll like it."

"Show me, Jack." Her eyelids grew heavy with lust. "Show me how much I'll like it."

CHAPTER 13
ADA

What was wrong with me? It was a loaded question I couldn't even begin to dissect.

Tonight was...educational. I was getting slapped in the face with a lot of hard truths about myself. Like how I was immune to fire, and getting tongue fucked in a stockade was a turn-on. Same with being tied up with pumpkin leaves as an eight-foot pumpkin-headed monster man railed me from behind.

And how the prospect of going to Hell and technically becoming the devil's property wasn't such a scary thought.

Being with Jack felt right. Somehow, I just knew that feeling wouldn't go away. It didn't matter where we were.

Around him, I had blinders on. Jack's dangerously seductive aura and his unyielding grip held me captive.

His blazing eyes cut through the night. They filled me with a blinding inferno of need and wonder.

Discovering this monster had every intention of dragging me back to Hell with him should have been absolutely terrifying. But all that knowledge did was add fuel to my radical and all-consuming attraction to Jack Calloway.

Several seconds stretched on forever. Jack didn't move. He kept a hand wedged between us, caressing my entrance.

Holding me in the possessive yet gentle curve of his fingers. The cool night air crackled with blistering tension and the promise of pleasure.

His head illuminated our bodies, bathing us in a sinister glow of flickering amber light. He was insanely fit, all hard muscles and bulging veins.

He lay my body out delicately over a large fallen log that rested in a small clearing, where moonlight bathed the leaf-covered forest floor. Light blanketed me in strips of silver, and spindly shadows cast from the bare tree branches.

Jack took a step back to admire me, then emitted a gravelly hum as if a thought had just occurred to him.

I propped myself up on my elbows and arched a brow. "What is it?"

"A memory just came back to me. One of my favorite nights we'd spent here together."

"Which memory?"

"The night I pledged myself to you. I sealed the oath in blood. Then I dressed your naked form in the sacrifice's life force."

My breath caught in my chest. "That was in the story. You slayed a goat and wrote the black magic curse right on my skin."

At first, he seemed surprised. Then he threw his head back and laughed. "Black magic? Hardly. It was a protection spell to keep you safe since you insisted on us living in town to be near your mother. She had a drinking problem, so you felt it was your duty to keep your apothecary open in the market to pay her rent. All the men there coveted you, and when they couldn't have you, they turned cruel."

The flames in Jack's head died down, turning a lethal pale blue to match his timbre. "One tried to take you by force. Do you remember?"

I shook my head. I didn't remember. But this story was still painfully familiar. Maybe it wasn't just my soul that had reincarnated. Maybe it was my whole life.

"You stopped him with your magic. When you told me, I was so angry that I killed him. They never found his body. They never found out it was me. Things like that were easy to hide in those days. It was his blood I used to paint your body. Not a goat's."

Jack's demeanor rolled off of him, alive like his flames dancing with violence.

The pleasure that made his voice bend when he spoke of murdering that man and covering me in his blood should have been sickening. But holy Hell. All it did was light me up on the inside. I was burning. Panting from the heat.

He'd killed for me on more than one occasion. And he'd do it again.

I wanted him to do it again.

His tone dropped to almost a whisper that was so husky and guttural, the hairs on the back of my neck stood up. "Stay here. Don't move."

I blinked. "Wait. Where are you going?"

"Hunting."

Hunting? A shiver shot through me. What did that mean?

Before I could ask, he'd already turned and disappeared into the trees, leaving me alone with nothing but the moon for company.

I'd spent an entire eighteen years without knowing Jack, but after one night together, it felt like a lifetime. Now that he was gone, I felt empty again. It was harder to deal with the loneliness now that I'd tasted what it was like to have that hole filled.

Trees rustled, and a branch snapped somewhere in the distance, interrupting my thoughts. My gaze swung around, scanning the clearing's perimeter. There was no sign of the fiery grin.

But I couldn't shake the feeling that someone was here, watching me.

I sat up, my arms folding around my torso to shield my breasts. "Who's there?"

I didn't expect an answer, so when a familiar laugh echoed from the shadows, my blood went cold. The man stepped into the clearing with his arm outstretched. He was holding a gun, and he had the barrel pointed directly at my head.

Lucas.

Chapter 14
Ada

"Surprised to see me again?" Lucas cackled, cocking the gun's trigger with a gut-jerking *click*.

It was almost funny how fear hadn't been much of a factor for me tonight. I'd almost been raped, thrown in the stocks, and set on fire. Screwed by a pumpkin-headed ghost.

But looking down the barrel of that gun sent a spike of terror lancing through me.

I wasn't afraid of dying.

I was afraid of this creepy asshole being the one to send me to Hell and not Jack.

Lucas had ditched his Krueger glove, which seemed like a bad move since it had literally saved his life back in the pumpkin patch.

Where had he come from? Why had he conveniently shown up after Jack had left me alone?

Had he been following us?

My stomach churned when I noticed the way his pants hung loosely around his hips with his fly undone—he'd needed his right hand free.

I'd been right. Normally, I loved being right. Who didn't? And where the Hallow Hill Hicks were concerned, I was usually right. It's not like it was hard to predict their moves, especially when they barely had two brain cells to rub together between the lot of them.

This time, I hated being right.

I'd hit the nail on the head with my guess that Lucas would come crawling back. Someone like him was too stupid to follow basic survival instincts. His obsession with me seemed to suffocate any shred of reason he had inside himself.

He had come back to watch us. We'd probably been too distracted to notice him.

"Oh, don't bother covering up now," he sneered, waggling the gun's barrel at my chest. I've already seen everything. And I saw what you let that monster do to you."

"Do you have a death wish or something? When Jack finds you, he's going to kill you like he did the others." I spoke flatly, not a drop of emotion in my words. I didn't care if Lucas lived or died. So long as he had air in his lungs, I just wanted him the fuck away from me.

"Yeah, right. I've already proven that I'm smarter than that gourd for brains. I came back to shoot it, so I could get it off you."

"Even if bullets worked on ghosts, why in the fuck would you do that? You're the one who trapped me for him in the first place."

"Yeah. So he'd hurt you. You weren't supposed to like all the disgusting shit he did to you. Shoulda known Little Moore Whore would get wet for something so fucked. That's how your whole family is. Totally fucked in the head. Good for nothing but the hole between your legs."

My head swirled with rage, and my jaw tightened. "Why show yourself?"

I jerked my chin to his hand. "Looks like you had a good time with the only willing partner you'll ever have."

Luc's bloodshot eyes narrowed. Damn. He was still drunk.

"I came back for what you've been owing me for a long time."

I couldn't move. "You monster..."

"Then I should be right up your alley, shouldn't I?" he cackled, the sound humorless and cold. "That's Adaline Moore, though. Hell's little whore. Now spread your legs so I can give you a real man's cock."

My throat convulsed. Where was Jack? What was I supposed to do?

I'd fight Lucas with everything I had. I'd rather go to Hell and meet Jack there later than be caught beneath Lucas, his disgusting alcohol-laced grunts in my ear and his tiny weenie touching any part of me.

"Eat shit and die, Luca Lou," I taunted, using the pet name I knew struck a soft spot.

His lip curled, and he jabbed the gun in the air, waggling it at me. "I'm not going to tell you again, Ada. Spread your legs. If you're a good little slut for me, I might even let you live when I'm done with you."

Luc's mouth opened wide, but instead of the next sentence coming out, a little *"oomph"* blew from him. Then a stream of blood flowed from his lips and dribbled down his chin.

We both looked down to see Jack's arm sticking straight through his chest, flesh smeared red with Luc's blood. In my lover's fist, he had something dark and throbbing clutched between his fingers.

Luc's still beating heart. Holy fucking shit.

Jack's fiery grin flickered through the murky night, hovering over my bully's head. The gun fell to the forest floor with a crunch, leaves and twigs snapping from its weight. Jack raised his free hand and grabbed Luc by his hair, sliding him off his arm.

By the time the boy hit the ground, he was dead.

My monster glanced down at the lifeless body, smirking. "See you in Hell. I'll enjoy torturing you right alongside your ancestor."

Jack stepped over the corpse, watching me with a natural expression, his grin gone. "Are you alright?"

My gaze lifted from the bully who'd tormented me for years and settled on Jack. "Why did you leave me?"

"I told you. To hunt." He gestured to the body with his heart still in his hand. "I knew he was close. I was hoping to lead him away from you." He lifted his bloody fist. "Either way. I got what I was after."

I worried my lip. Luc's death didn't bother me. Instead, my nerves lit with dark excitement.

"Lay down, Ada," Jack instructed, gleaning my arousal by the way his voice went rough with hunger. "

I laid back on the log with my hands falling from my breasts to lace together over my navel. My eyes drifted shut. My muscles unwound as I felt his presence push closer, his demeanor swaddling me like a heated blanket.

My eyes shot open when I felt a drop of something warm and wet fall between the globes of my breasts. Holy shit.

My eyelashes fluttered as Jack squeezed his fist, and more of Luc's blood peppered my torso.

He was covering me in Luc's blood... I should have been horrified and disgusted. Not turned on. Being turned on wasn't the normal reaction. But hey, fuck normal. This night had confirmed I wasn't anything close to normal, and for the first time, I was okay with that. I was done beating myself up for who I was. By feeding into that bullshit, I was doing exactly what I hated everyone else for. I was done being anything but proud of the witchy, kinky, Hell-bound freak that I was.

Jack squeezed until all the blood had been emptied from the

organ and tossed it aside in the grass. He smoothed his hands over me, smearing the blood around.

He began to draw runes in the blood, and my breath caught when he recited the last lines of the poem I'd heard so many times before.

"Forever mine, forevermore, through dust and darkest ash."

Chapter 15
Ada

Crusted in the blood of my bully, I felt like some dark goddess of the woods.

And Jack worshipped me, switching from the poem to murmuring strings of unintelligible verses in that demonic tongue.

"Are you casting a spell on me?"

"An incantation for protection." His voice dropped, coming out hard and withdrawn. "Just in case you choose to stay behind."

"How many times do I have to tell you that I choose you?"

He said nothing as he straddled the log and slid me closer so that our centers met. I hooked my legs around his waist on instinct, and a moan pushed past my lips as he braced his hands on the log on either side of my head, arching over me.

"One more time," he said. "Always one more time."

My heart squeezed. I felt so warm in the wake of his flames. "I choose you."

He gazed hungrily into my eyes, his fire consuming me from the inside out. Leaning on one forearm, he took his free hand and trailed it down my torso. Luc's blood was still wet and smeared all the way down to the top line of my pubic hair.

Jack reached between us and grabbed the base of his cock.

He seemed so eager, so greedy for more of what he'd already tasted. His fingers shook as he rubbed his cock up and down the apex of my center. "Already wet for me."

When he sunk into me with one long stroke, I screamed.

"And so *tight*," he groaned on a fragmented breath that shot through my core, making my tummy muscles clench.

When he sunk into me with one long stroke, I screamed.

He wasn't slow or gentle like he had been the first time. He pounded me ruthlessly.

"Harder, faster. Split me apart."

Jack's hellish laughter echoed through my skull, and something inside me snapped. My desire for him exploded into a roaring need.

"Look at you," he crooned down at me, muscles rippling beneath his sweat-soaked skin in the light of his flames. "Getting plowed so prettily."

My eyes widened with shock, and my pulse froze as I watched vines burst from his back like freaking Dr. Octopus. Oh my God. This magic wasn't just summoning some alien-like pumpkin vines out of the ground. *They were a part of him.*

I was practically drooling as the vines crept over my body, twisting at my breasts and tugging my arms over my head.

"Choke me," I moaned, practically begging.

Jack's pleased hum sunk straight to the place where we were joined.

"Fuck. You're so goddamn sinful. I'm going to send you straight to Hell, Adaline Moore, wrapped in a pretty little bow."

The leafy green tendrils coiled around my throat and applied enough pressure to have me seeing two of him.

Something inside my walls twisted and pulsed, expanding, stretching me wider. "Wh–what's happening?"

"My stem, it's swelling in the middle, keeping me locked inside your sweet cunt, little witch."

Holy Hell. He was talking about a knot. I'd read about knots in monster romance and monster porn videos, but I don't know why I hadn't considered the possibility that Jack could do that.

He sat heavily inside me, the tip of his member curling like the tip of a pumpkin stem and coming to rest against that spot inside me that had me writhing in ecstasy.

The orgasm came suddenly, brutally. It tore through me, breaking me asunder, and fuck me, was the ride intense. Euphoric waves of bliss crashed over me, leaving me gasping as he came moments later.

He loomed over me, looking so monstrous...and all mine.

In a soft moment that took me by surprise, he swept a lock of my hair out of my eyes.

"You burn so brightly for me, Adaline Moore."

WE LAY in each other's arms until the light in the sky grew brighter, hues of purple and orange peeking through the tree branches and the darkness fading. Jack's flames dimmed.

"What's happening to you?"

For the first time tonight, he looked sad. His grin was nowhere in sight, and his flames simmered low. "The door between the realm of the living and the dead is closing. I have to go back."

"Are you going to take me with you?"

"You'll be giving your life up here."

"I don't have a life here." It wasn't until one of his vines swiped across my cheek to wipe a tear that I realized I was crying. "I want to be with you. You said you were taking my soul. Take the rest of me too."

There was that smile again, creeping back. He reached for me with his hand this time and caressed my chin in the cradle of his palm. "Such a good girl. Such a lovely little witch. It would be selfish to take you to Hell with me."

The sigh he gave was throaty and rough and turned to a growl as his sweet smile turned sinister. "But... It's as I said. I'm not the prince from all the stories. I'm the monster."

He took a few steps backward. I watched in complete awe as he stuck his fingers in his mouth and retracted them a beat later, their tips on fire like matches. Then he drew a curving line in the air as if tracing an archway.

The flame struck a line of flickering flames in the shape of a doorway that hovered in midair. The door opened, but I couldn't see anything inside through all the smoke.

"I don't give a shit if I'm taking the last light in this godforsaken town. They can rot in darkness. You're mine. My heart's flame. My everything. I've waited four hundred years to find you again."

He stretched his hand out, and I stared at it for a moment before taking it tentatively, feeling sure but nervous all at the same time. I mean, here I was, about to step through Hell's gate.

Despite how intense and monumental this single moment was, I found myself laughing. "It's strange, isn't it? They told me my whole life that I was a witch and I was going to burn in Hell. I didn't think they'd be so right."

Jack pulled me against his hard chest, taking my face between his hands and leveling me with his flaming gaze. My body tensed, and my thighs pulsed with that familiar heat he could ignite with a single look.

"They are all damned."

My gaze trailed past his shoulder to gape into the gate. "Like us..."

He wrenched my gaze back, forcing my attention on him. "No. Nothing like us. They will burn like they burned us. It will be their agony. And their screams will be our fucking bliss."

He grinned. "So come with me, Adaline Moore. Come with me to Hell. Not to die. But so we can finally live."

He walked me to the gate, and we paused just before the fiery arch.

Holy shit. I was going to Hell.

But...I still wasn't scared. Not with Jack by my side. In the end, I was ending up with my childhood crush. My darkest fantasies had come to life. And in my darkest hour, on the most haunted night of the year, I'd solved a mystery that had hung over my family's head for four centuries.

Jack was real. It didn't really matter if I was the reincarnation of the original Adaline Moore. Jack was mine. And I was his.

I'd finally found my escape from this godforsaken town. In Hell. Who knew exactly what was going to happen once we stepped through the gate? But there was a thrill in the unknown of it all.

Whatever lay in wait on the other side, through dust and darkest ash, we'd survive.

With one last glance back at Jack, I squeezed his hand, holding him tight, and stepped through the arch into Hell.

Where witches were welcome.

Where dark deals were born.

Where I could burn as bright as I was always meant to.

Where I would burn for all eternity for Jack.

The End

www.ingramcontent.com/pod-product-compliance
Ingram Content Group UK Ltd.
Pitfield, Milton Keynes, MK11 3LW, UK
UKHW020041050925
7726UKWH00073B/983